Pooh's Best Friend

Disney's
Winnie the Pooh First Readers

Pooh Gets Stuck
Bounce, Tigger, Bounce!
Pooh's Pumpkin
Rabbit Gets Lost
Pooh's Honey Tree
Happy Birthday, Eeyore!
Pooh's Best Friend

Disney's
A Winnie the Pooh First Reader

Pooh's Best Friend

Ann Braybrooks
ILLUSTRATED BY Tim Jones

DISNEY
PRESS

NEW YORK

Pooh's Best Friend

One fine spring day,
Winnie the Pooh
got to thinking about friends.
He had many friends.
But who was his *best* friend?

Could it be Owl?

Eeyore?

Or Rabbit?

Tigger?

Kanga?

Or Roo?

And what about Piglet?

Hmm, Pooh thought.

What is a best friend?

I think I shall ask everyone

in the Hundred-Acre Wood.

Pooh licked some honey
from a honeypot,
then headed outside.

First, Pooh asked Owl.

"Owl, what is a best friend?"

"My Great-Aunt Gabby once said,

'A best friend is someone

you can talk to about anything.'"

said Owl.

Pooh and Owl talked about
some things.
They talked about the weather
and Owl's relatives.
But Pooh and Piglet
talked about everything.
They talked about hunting
heffalumps and finding honey.
They talked about the best places
for a picnic.

Next, Pooh asked Rabbit.

"Rabbit, what is a best friend?"

"If you must know,"
replied Rabbit,
"a best friend is someone
who is unselfish."

Pooh liked Rabbit.

But was Rabbit as unselfish as Piglet?

Pooh remembered

all the unselfish things

that Piglet had done for him.

He let Pooh sit by the fire

in his favorite chair.

He gave Pooh the biggest slice

of huckleberry pie.

Next, Pooh asked Eeyore.

"Eeyore, what is a best friend?"

"I wouldn't know, Pooh.

But I suspect it's someone

who remembers your birthday."

Pooh wondered if Eeyore
had ever remembered his birthday.
Once Piglet had thrown
a party for Pooh,
complete with balloons and cake
and honey lemonade.

Next, Pooh asked Tigger.

"Tigger, what is a best friend?"

"Hoo-hoo-*hoo*! That's easy,"
Tigger said.

"A best friend is someone
who sticks around,
even if you bounce him
accidentally."

Hmm, Pooh thought.

I stick around Tigger

when he bounces me.

Then Pooh remembered all the times
that Piglet had stuck around.
Like the time Pooh
had forgotten
to meet Piglet
at the bridge.
And the time
that Pooh had eaten
Piglet's lunch by mistake.

Next, Pooh asked Kanga.

"Kanga, what is a best friend?"

"A best friend, Pooh dear,

is someone who is patient

and kind," said Kanga.

Pooh thought,

that sounds like Kanga.

But then Pooh thought
a little longer.

Kanga had also described Piglet.

Piglet was all of those things
and more.

Piglet was easy to talk to.

He was unselfish and loyal.

And he always remembered
Pooh's birthday.

As Pooh turned to go,

Roo squeaked,

"I know what a best friend is!

A best friend is someone

who asks you to play!"

"You're right, Roo," said Pooh.

"Thank you!"

At that moment, Pooh knew

who his best friend was—Piglet.

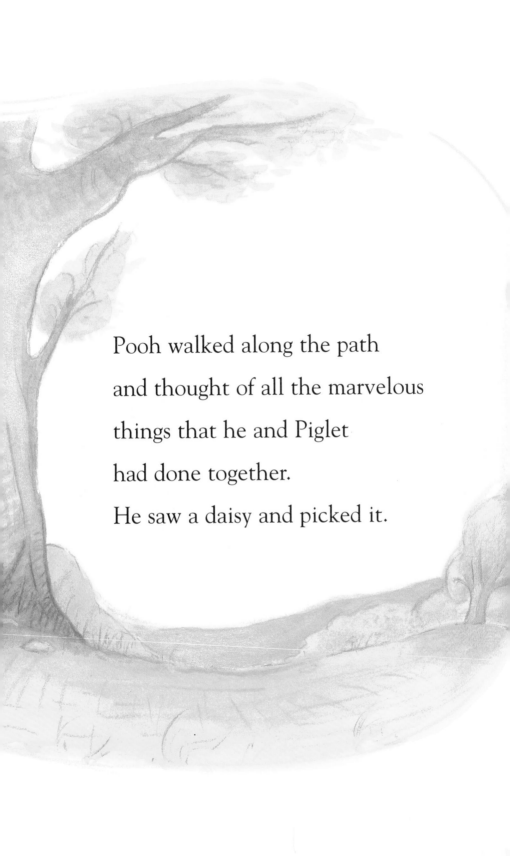

Pooh walked along the path
and thought of all the marvelous
things that he and Piglet
had done together.
He saw a daisy and picked it.

He hurried to Piglet's house
and thumped on the door.
"Hello, Piglet!" said Pooh.
"I brought you a daisy."
"How kind of you,"
said Piglet.
"Would you like a piece
of huckleberry pie?"

The two friends sat inside.
But this time, Pooh insisted
that Piglet sit by the fire
in the comfiest chair
and take the biggest piece
of huckleberry pie.

For if Piglet was Pooh's best friend,
Pooh wanted to be his.

Join the Pooh Friendship Club

A wonder-filled year of friendly activities and interactive fun for your child!

The fun starts with:

- Clubhouse play kit
- Exclusive club T-shirt
- The first issue of "Pooh News"
- Toys, stickers and gifts from Pooh

The fun goes on with:

- Quarterly issues of "Pooh News" each with special surprises
- Birthday and Friendship Day cards from Pooh
- And more!

Join now and also get a colorful, collectible Pooh art print

Yearly membership costs just $25 plus 15 Hunny Pot Points. (Look for Hunny Pot Points on Pooh products.)

To join, send check or money order and Hunny Pot Points to:

Pooh Friendship Club
P.O. Box 1723
Minneapolis, MN 55440-1723

Please include the following information: Parent name, child name, complete address, phone number, sex (M/F), child's birthday, and child's T-shirt size (S, M, L)
(CA and MN residents add applicable sales tax.)

Call toll-free for more information
1-888-FRNDCLB

You're a Real Friend

Fun for kids ages 3-

Pooh Friendship Club

Help your child learn MATH and READING with a computer and a silly old bear.

©Disney

Disney's Learning Series on CD-ROM

...our child on the path to success in the 100 Acre Wood,
...Pooh and his friends make learning math and reading
...isney's Ready for Math with Pooh helps kids learn all the
...tant basics, including patterns, sequencing, counting,
...eginning addition & subtraction. In Disney's Ready to
...with Pooh, kids learn all the fundamentals including the
...bet, phonics, and spelling simple words. Filled with
...ing activities and rich learning environments, the 100
...Wood is a delightful world for your child to explore
...nd over. Discover the magic of learning with Pooh.

NEW! Disney's **Learning Series**

Once Again The Magic Of Disney Begins With a Mouse

Disney INTER ACTIVE

Wonderfully Whimsical Ways To Bring Winnie The Pooh Into Your Child's Life

Pooh FRIENDSHIP

Pooh and the gang help children learn about liking each other for who they are in 5 charming volumes about what it means to be a friend.

Pooh STORYBOOK CLASSICS

These 4 enchanting volumes let you share the original A.A. Milne stories — first shown in theaters — you so fondly remember from your own childhood.

Pooh PLAYTIME

Children can't help but play and pretend with Pooh and his friends in 5 playful volumes that celebrate the joys of being young.

Pooh LEARNING

Pooh and his pals help children discover sharing and caring in 5 loving volumes about growing up.

FREE*
Flash Cards Attached!
A Different Set With Each
Pooh Learning Video!
* With purchase, while supplies last.